# You Don't Belong Here

ISBN 978-1-64492-371-9 (paperback)
ISBN 978-1-64492-372-6 (digital)

Christian Faith Publishing, Inc.
832 Park Avenue
Meadville, PA 16335
www.christianfaithpublishing.com

Printed in the United States of America

# You Don't Belong Here

Written by Sean O'Toole

With Illustrations by
Pamela Nicosia

Two muskrats named Marty and Manny were brothers. What's a muskrat, you ask? Muskrats are small animals that look similar to a beaver except they have long rat-like tails. They also live near water and are very good at digging holes with their sharp claws. In other words, they make a big mess wherever they go, especially if it's in someone's backyard or garden. Anyway, there was a big flood in Marty and Manny's home, so they were forced away by the flooding into old Mrs. Jenkin's backyard, where she just so happened to have a beautiful vegetable garden. And take a guess what muskrats love to eat? Yup, you guessed it. Vegetables.

Mrs. Jenkins didn't mind at first. She thought they were kinda cute. But then she started to realize how much of a mess they were making, digging their holes all over her backyard. And they were gobbling up all her veggies and tearing up her lawn. They were not making good pets at all.

She had finally had enough of these two trouble-making muskrats. So she picked up the phone and called Paulie's Pest Control to try and remove them from her yard. Paulie placed out two box traps with some bait inside to try and catch them. He promised Mrs. Jenkins that he would not hurt the animals. He would just catch them and relocate them to a new home.

Later that day Marty and Manny saw the yummy bait in the trap, and Marty wasted no time and ran right into the trap and got caught.

"Oh no!" said Manny.

Paulie quickly came to take him away.

Manny ran back into his hole and sadly watched as Paulie took away his brother.

Mrs. Jenkins then came outside, pointed her finger at Marty in the cage, and said, "Sorry, little guy, but you don't belong here."

9

Paulie drove with Marty far away to a forest area with a little pond nearby. Paulie placed the cage down on the ground and let Marty go. He drove off, leaving Marty all alone. Marty was scared. He had never been without his brother before. And now he was in a strange place by himself. He quickly dug a little hole under a bush for himself, then ran off to get a drink from the pond. He was really thirsty.

Marty took a long drink from the pond, and when he turned around, he was surrounded by other animals! Standing there staring at him was a goose, a chipmunk, two squirrels, two ducks, and a smelly old skunk.

The goose stepped up and said, "What are you supposed to be?"

With a puzzled face, Marty said, "I'm a muskrat."

The chipmunk quickly ran up to Marty, looked him up and down, and said, "He's funny looking," in a squeaky little voice.

"Yeah, he doesn't belong here," said one of the ducks.

All the other animals started nodding in agreement when suddenly the skunk yelled, "Everybody, run! Here comes Ronny!"

All the animals scattered in different directions as a vicious-looking raccoon slowly approached. The goose and the ducks jumped into the pond and swam away. The chipmunk ran and ducked quickly into its little hole in the ground. The skunk jumped behind a bush and sprayed a bit of its stinky smell all around it. And the squirrels ran to climb a tree, but on the way, one of the squirrels tripped and hurt its leg!

Marty saw what happened and quickly dragged the injured animal into the hole he had made earlier just as the raccoon's claw tried to swipe at them. Ronny couldn't reach far enough into the deep hole to grab them.

"I'll get you next time!" snarled the raccoon as he ran back off into the forest.

Once the coast was clear, all the animals came out of hiding. The injured squirrel looked up at Marty and said, "Thanks for saving me. My name is Sara, and this is my brother Stewey. We're squirrels, which means we're really good climbers."

Marty nodded and said, "You're welcome. My name is Marty. And who was that big scary guy?"

The goose came waddling over and said, "That was Ronny the raccoon. He is very dangerous and has been trying to make one of us his next meal. My name is Gary, and I'm a goose, which means I can swim and fly."

Next, the skunk walked over. "My name is Sammy, short for Samantha, and I'm a skunk, which means I'm really good at digging like you. But I can also spray a stinky smell to scare off nasty animals like Ronny."

Marty looked amazed and said, "Wow! I wish I could do that!"

Then the little chipmunk ran over and said in a squeaky voice, "My name is Charlie, and I'm a chipmunk."

Marty looked at Charlie and said, "I've seen chipmunks before. You guys are super fast!"

Charlie smiled.

Last, but not least, the two ducks waddled over. "Hello, I'm Davey, and this is my sister Dottie, and we're ducks. Similar to Gary the goose but smaller. We can swim and fly too. Sorry, we weren't very friendly to you earlier. We don't get too many strangers here at the pond."

Marty shrugged and said, "No problem. I understand."

Gary the goose stepped forward again and said, "We've been trying to hatch a plan to stop Ronny the raccoon from terrorizing us. Any ideas?"

Marty thought for a moment and said, "Well, me and my brother Manny used to play tag and set traps for each other by digging holes in the ground, then covering the holes with leaves and sticks so we wouldn't see them and fall into them. Maybe we can dig a hole and give that a try?"

All the animals looked at each other in agreement that this was a good idea.

Gary stepped up and said, "That's actually a really good idea, Marty, but we're going to need somebody to lure Ronny into the trap."

They all looked at each other. Nobody wanted to be the bait.

Marty realized this and stood up confidently and said, "I'll do it. I'll be the bait. He's extra mad at me for saving Sara earlier, so he'll definitely come after me."

All the animals were impressed with Marty's bravery.

With no time to waste, the animals got started on the first part of their plan right away. Stewey the squirrel agreed to be the lookout to make sure Ronny didn't show up early. Marty and Sammy the skunk started digging the giant hole deep enough to catch the raccoon.

Meanwhile, Gary the goose and the two ducks, Davey and Dottie, searched along the shoreline for sticks to help cover the hole once completed. And little Charlie the chipmunk ran around as fast as he could, picking up leaves to throw on top of the sticks. They all chipped in and were able to make the perfect trap in no time at all.

So now that the trap was set, the next step was lure Ronny the raccoon to the bait. All the animals began to quack, chirp, and squeak as loud as they could. This immediately got Ronny's attention. Stewie ran quickly back up the tree for a look, saw him coming, and yelled, "Here he comes!"

Quickly, all the animals hid away. Everyone except for Marty who stood bravely right in front of the trap. He could hear Dave and Dottie say at the same time, "Be careful, Marty!" in the distance.

Ronny saw Marty and approached him slowly, snarling, "Looks like you're all alone now. Let's find out just how tasty you are." And Ronny ran at Marty as fast as he could.

Marty was getting nervous but stood his ground until the last second. Then he turned around, quickly jumped over the trap, as Ronny kept running after him. Then *swoosh*!

Down the hole Ronny fell. The trap had worked! Marty let out a sigh of relief. All the animals came out of hiding and cheered.

Ronny was deep down the hole, yelling, "Help me! I broke my leg!"

Gary looked down the hole and said, "Why should we help you? All you've ever done is try to eat us!"

Ronny looked up at Gary sadly and said, "But you guys are all food for raccoons. What else am I supposed to eat?"

All the animals shrugged. They weren't sure what other foods a raccoon might want to eat.

Then Sammy the skunk remembered that she had seen some other raccoons eating berries on a nearby bush once. So she ran quickly to the bush and broke off a branch full of berries. She came back to the hole and threw the branch down to Ronny.

"Try eating these. See if you like them," she said.

Ronny tried a few berries off the branch and said, "Wow, these are really good! I guess I could get used to eating those."

Sammy smiled and said, "That's great! Because there's plenty to go around!"

All the animals huddled together to discuss whether or not to help Ronny out of the hole.

Gary waddled back over to the hole and said, "We've decided to help you out if you promise never to try and eat any of us again."

Ronny agreed.

Stewey the squirrel ran off and found a long vine that the animals could use as a rope to try and pull Ronny out of the hole.

"Tie the vine to your body, and we'll pull you up out of there," yelled Gary.

All the animals then grabbed the vine and pulled as hard as they could. The raccoon was well fed, so he was super heavy.

"Good thing you'll be going on a diet soon!" Charlie the chipmunk said in his squeaky voice.

Finally, thanks to the teamwork, they were able to successfully pull him out of the hole.

Ronny said, "Thank you, everybody. And I'm sorry about everything. I promise never to try and hurt any of you again." He laid down and started munching on some berries while Sammy was nice enough to tend to his broken leg.

Everyone turned to Marty and thanked him for his help and bravery. They all happily agreed that Marty does indeed belong at the pond and is most welcome to stay. That made Marty smile.

Just then, they heard a loud noise behind them and turned around to see a truck door open and shut. It was Paulie's Pest Control with another box trap! He had finally caught Marty's brother, Manny, and was letting him go!

The brothers were reunited at last. Marty brought Manny over and introduced him to all his new friends. They were all very happy to meet him. The muskrat brothers finally found a new home at the pond where they now truly belonged.

The End

# About the Author

Sean O'Toole was born in Baldwin, New York, a small town on Long Island. He's one of four children with three sisters. Sean still lives on Long Island in a town named Farmingdale. He works as a pest control operator and has a lovely wife named Cathy, a teen stepson named Tristan, and two wonderful boys of his own named Dylan and Brayden. *You Don't Belong Here* is the first book Sean has ever written. He got the idea for this book after finding two muskrats at a customer's house in Long Beach, New York, and realizing how peculiar they looked and how much damage they can cause to a backyard. Sean dedicates this book to his sons Dylan and Brayden.

CPSIA information can be obtained
at www.ICGtesting.com
Printed in the USA
BVHW020102250419
546508BV00009B/19/P